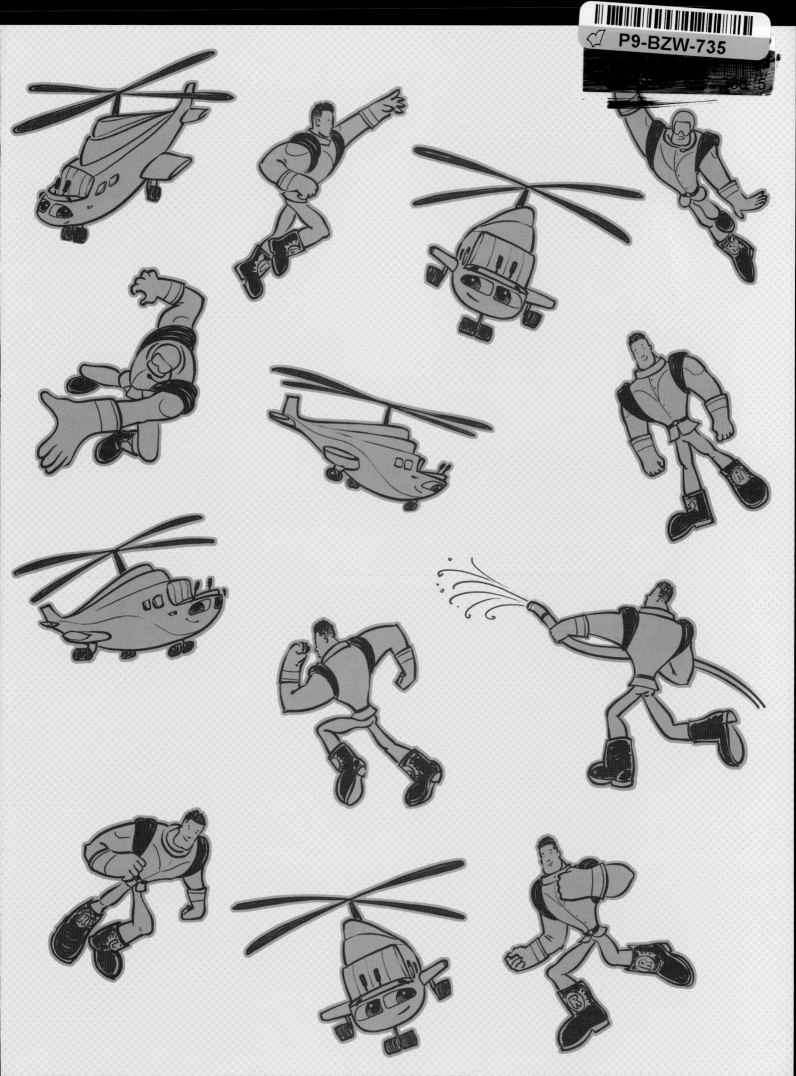

For my favorite helicopter pilot, Eliot Sprague,
with gratitude
—SDR

To Anthony Jr. and Amani,
my superheroes
—DT

About This Book

The illustrations for this book were rendered digitally using Clip Studio Paint, Procreate, and Photoshop. This book was edited by Deirdre Jones and designed by Patrick Collins with art direction from Saho Fujii. The production was supervised by Patricia Alvarado, and the production editor was Marisa Finkelstein. The text was set in Andika, and the display type is Air Millhouse.

ROTO and ROy
HELICOPTER HEROES

SHERRI DUSKEY RINKER

Illustrated by DON TATE

L B
LITTLE, BROWN AND COMPANY
New York Boston

As the sun begins to rise,
brightening the morning skies:

Thud-thud-thud-thud-thud!

The sound of footsteps on the run,
as big boots rush toward Hangar One.

RRRRRRRRRR!

Steel-gray doors open wide,
and there sits Roto, right inside.
She's fueled and ready, brave and strong.
Her shiny wings are tough and long.
Superhero helicopter!
She's awesome, and *nothing* can stop her.

With fists on hips, and massive height,
Big Roy Thunder blocks the light.
Like a mountain, there he stands.
"Let's ROCK, my friend!" He *thwacks* his hands.

He strides toward Roto

and climbs in,

right to the cockpit, to begin.
"Big emergency out there—
we have to go, no time to spare!"
By radio, she hears Roy say,
"Roy and Roto—on our way!"

With Pilot Roy securely in,
a button's pushed, and rotors spin.
Roy works the pedals and the sticks.
Roto's ready! And... *she lifts*!

Rising, rising, up—up—up!

Faster! **Whup-Whup-Whup-Whup-Whup!**

Blades are whirling, all a blur,

but this is easy work for her!

Moving quickly, soaring high,

two heroes head into the sky.

Roy says, "This job—it'll be rough.
Good thing, Roto, you're so tough."
Up ahead, smoke fills the air.
"We are heading over there.

"Lightning struck the canyon ground,
and fires started all around.
That's our mission, that's our role:
to get those flames under control!"

Roto nods and picks up speed,
ready to help when there is need.
She heads into the heat and haze,
off to work, to fight the blaze.

Roto pushes toward a lake.
Her hose is dropping, for intake.
The wind is whipping hard and fast,
and giant waves are pushing past.

But Roto doesn't hesitate—
she hovers low and keeps it straight.
Roy holds on tight, so they don't spin,
and Roto sucks the water in.

With nerves of steel, they're strong and smart.
Both Roy and Roto do their part:
One thousand gallons in the hold,
because they're steady, calm, and bold.

Together, these two work as one.
Superheroes *get it done*!

Whirrrrrrrr!

Now *heavy*, Roto powers through.
She knows just what she has to do.

She grits her teeth. She's working hard.
The flames snap up—she stays on guard.

Roy Thunder guides her from his seat,
through the high winds, smoke, and heat.

It's hard to see—the air is black—
but they hold firm, no turning back:
Roy steers through smoke and over flames.
Roto's ready! And...*she aims*!
Flames scorch her, but she doesn't stop.
She dumps the water right on top!

Fires smolder—then reignite,
the heroes don't give up the fight.
Fill up and make another run,
they won't stop until they're done.
Ten more times they go around,
dumping water on the ground.

Finally, when they look about,
they see that all the flames are *out*!
"BOOM!" says Roy (his trademark shout).
"THAT'S what I'm TALKIN' about!"

BOOM!

But wait!
Something's moving in the brush.
The team moves closer in a rush....
A poor stray dog! It might be hurt,
hobbling through the ash and dirt.
It's on a cliff, and it might fall!
There's not much time to help at all!

Without one word between the two,
they're ready for . . . *an air rescue!*
As Roto hovers straight and low,
Roy gears up, all set to go.
He rides the long, long cable down.
It takes him to the hazy ground.

The puppy soon crawls out to see
and jumps right onto Big Roy's knee.
"You aren't hurt at all—just scared!
Don't worry, pup, you're in good care."
As Roy Thunder holds the pup,
Roto pulls hard and lifts them up.

Once they're safely back inside,
Roto lifts and starts to glide.
The pup is safe. The fire's out.
Roy Thunder gives another shout,
"BOOM! Roto, you're AWESOMESAUCE!
You're the best! You are THE BOSS!

Roto proudly nods *thank you!*
She's heading homeward with her crew.

Woof! Woof!

The pup is happy as can be.
The flying *duo* is now *three*!

Now Roto, Roy—and little Red—
head toward home and head to bed.
Knowing they have done their best,
they'll settle down and get some rest.

Until…they get another call
and jump to action, one and all.
They'll be *up*, without delay,
ready to go, to save the day.
To fly wherever there is need—
they're superheroes! Yes, indeed.

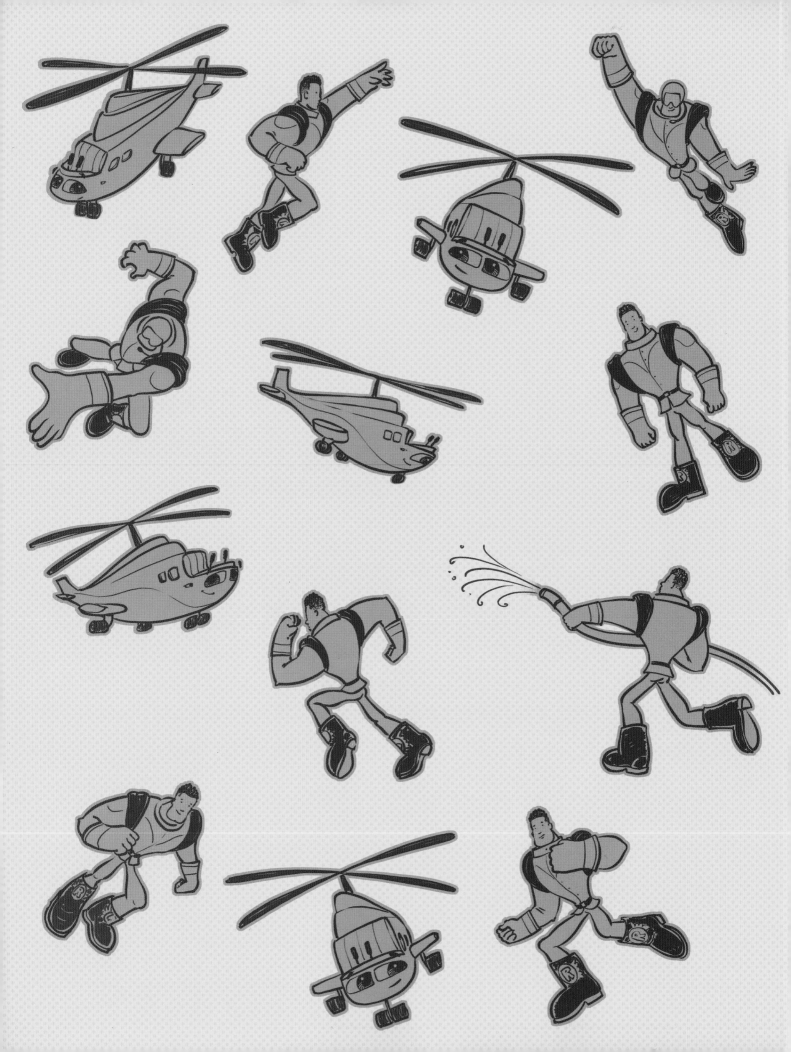